The Bramble

written by Lee Nordling

illustrated by Bruce Zick

Carolrhoda Books / Minneapolis

Special thanks to editor Andrew Karre, who helped make the story better. This is for Cheri, the love of all of my lives.

—Lee Nordling

For my wife Anja and Daughter Isabella who reopened my eyes to worlds of wonder.

—Bruce Zick

Story and script © 2013 by Lee Nordling
Illustrations copyright © 2013 by Bruce Zick

Carolrhoda Books
A division of Lerner Publishing Group, Inc.
241 First Avenue North
Minneapolis, MN 55401 U.S.A.
Website address: www.lernerbooks.com

Library of Congress Cataloging-in-Publication Data available.
ISBN 978-0-7613-5856-5

Manufactured in the United States of America
1 - DP - 7/15/13

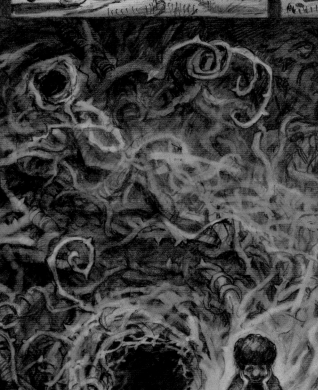